Marvin

shapes up

by Tom Armstrong

A BYRON PREISS
VISUAL PUBLICATIONS INC. BOOK

PUBLISHED BY POCKET BOOKS NEW YORK

Another *Original* publication of POCKET BOOKS

The comic strips in this book have been
previously published in syndication.

POCKET BOOKS, a division of Simon & Schuster, Inc.
1230 Avenue of the Americas, New York, N.Y. 10020

ISBN: 0-671-60706-5

First Pocket Books trade paperback printing May, 1987

10 9 8 7 6 5 4 3 2 1

MARVIN and logo are trademarks of News America Syndicate.

POCKET and colophon are registered trademarks
of Simon & Schuster, Inc.

Printed in the U.S.A.

Marvin Books

Marvin Steps Out
Marvin: Born to Be Wild
Marvin Spoil Me
Marvin Shapes Up

Published by POCKET BOOKS

MARVIN'S

10 STEP
SHAPE-UP

P R O G R A M

STEP 1

The Warm Up

BEFORE ATTEMPTING ANY STRENUOUS EXERCISE PROGRAM, IT IS IMPORTANT THAT YOU START WITH A FEW STRETCHING WARM UPS TO AVOID MUSCLE CRAMPS.

STEP 2

Arms/Chest Exercise

HOLD A JAR OF BABY FOOD
FIRMLY IN YOUR LEFT HAND.
THEN, USING YOUR RIGHT HAND,
GRASP THE LID AND TWIST IT
SLOWLY IN A COUNTER-
CLOCKWISE DIRECTION. NOW
HOLD A SPOON WITH YOUR
RIGHT HAND AND EMPTY THE
CONTENTS INTO YOUR MOUTH.

STEP 3

Lung Exercise

MOST OF TODAY'S MEDICAL EXPERTS RECOGNIZE THE IMPORTANCE OF INCREASING THE LUNGS' EFFICIENCY AT TAKING IN OXYGEN. THIS BREATHING EXERCISE MAY BE PERFORMED IN SEVERAL DIFFERENT POSITIONS.

(SEE ILLUSTRATIONS)

POSITION A.

POSITION B.

POSITION C.

STEP 4
Proper Diet

JUST REMEMBER THE OLD NUTRITIONAL AXIOM: "YOU ARE WHAT YOU EAT." NOW, WHICH WOULD YOU RATHER BE, A STEAMED VEGETABLE OR A RICH HUNK?

STEP 5
Gymnastics

THIS NEXT EXERCISE IS A VARIATION OF THE PARALLEL BARS. FROM A STANDING POSITION, PLACE BOTH HANDS ON THE RAIL *(ILLUS.1)*. THEN SWING YOUR LEGS, ONE AT A TIME, OVER THE RAIL *(ILLUS.2)*. DISMOUNT TO THE FLOOR *(ILLUS.3)* AND RUN TO THE COOKIE JAR BEFORE ANYONE NOTICES YOU'RE MISSING *(ILLUS.4)*.

(ILLUS.1)

(ILLUS.2)

(ILLUS.3)

(ILLUS.4)

STEP 6

Waistline Exercise

STAND UP STRAIGHT AND PUT YOUR RIGHT HAND ON YOUR HIP. NOW GRASP YOUR WAIST AND PULL. IF YOU CAN PINCH MORE THAN AN INCH OF FAT, YOU KNOW YOU HAVE PLENTY OF ROOM FOR SOME COOKIES OR ICE CREAM.

STEP 7

Buttocks Exercise

FOR THIS EXERCISE, LIE ON YOUR BACK WITH YOUR LEGS EXTENDED UP IN THE AIR. THEN KICK VIGOROUSLY. REPEAT THIS ROUTINE AT LEAST 20 TIMES A DAY.

NOTE: THIS EXERCISE WILL REQUIRE THE ASSISTANCE OF A PARTNER.

STEP 8

Abdominal Exercise

THIS SIMPLE ISOMETRIC EXERCISE CAN BE PERFORMED WHILE SEATED AT A TABLE. BY FLEXING YOUR ABDOMINAL MUSCLES, TRY TO PUSH THE TABLE AWAY FROM YOU. IF, HOWEVER, YOUR STOMACH HANGS *OVER* THE TABLE, THEN IT'S TIME TO PUSH *YOURSELF* AWAY.

STEP 9
Aerobics

BY SPEEDING UP YOUR HEART'S METABOLIC RATE FOR AN EXTENDED PERIOD OF TIME, AEROBIC EXERCISE ENABLES YOUR BODY TO BURN OFF EXCESS CALORIES. TELEVISION VIDEOS ARE OFTEN USED IN AEROBICS.

STEP 10
The Cool Down

AFTER FINISHING EACH
WORKOUT, IT'S IMPORTANT
THAT YOU DON'T NEGLECT
YOUR COOL DOWN. THE
COOL DOWN HELPS RESTORE
YOUR CIRCULATION TO PRE-
EXERCISE LEVELS SO
THAT YOU FEEL RELAXED.

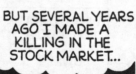

THIS ARTICLE SAYS THAT PEOPLE WHO SPEND A LOT OF TIME TOGETHER START LOOKING ALIKE

Tom Armstrong

I DON'T THINK THAT'S TRUE, DO, YOU, FLOPPET?

MARVIN'S BUNNY HAS A NAME!! MS. KRIS NIEWOLNY OF FRANKLIN, WISCONSIN, WAS CHOSEN AS THE GRAND PRIZE WINNER FOR HER ENTRY OF "FLOPPET" IN MARVIN'S NAME THE BUNNY CONTEST CONGRATULATIONS, KRIS, AND A BIG THANKS FROM MARVIN TO EVERYONE WHO ENTERED!

SLURP! SLURP!

BLECCH! THIS MILK HAS AN ARTIFICIAL AFTERTASTE

THE COW THAT GAVE IT MUST HAVE GRAZED ON ASTROTURF

Tom Armstrong

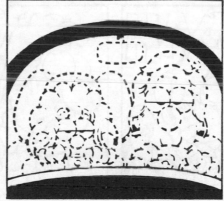

WITH THIS NEW OUTFIT, I'M ALL SET FOR A REALLY GOOD WORKOUT

YOU CAN ALWAYS TELL WHEN SOMEONE'S NOT VERY SERIOUS ABOUT EXERCISING

THEY BUY SWEATSUITS THAT ARE "DRYCLEAN ONLY"

TOM ARMSTRONG

YOUR MOTHER AND I REALIZE THAT YOU'RE JUST A BABY, MARVIN...

SO WE TRY TO MAKE ALLOWANCES FOR YOU WHEN YOU DO THINGS LIKE THIS

WOW! THEY'RE GOING TO START PAYING ME FOR MAKING MESSES

TOM ARMSTRONG

DO ALL YOU SQUIRRELS STAY UP NORTH DURING THE WINTER?

ALL EXCEPT FOR MY UNCLE SIDNEY

HE ALWAYS GOES TO FLORIDA FOR THE SEASON

ISN'T THAT KIND OF A LONG WALK?

NOT FOR SIDNEY, HE'S A FLYING SQUIRREL

BRRRTT

ALL RIGHT, WHO'S THE WISE GUY WHO PUT THE WHOOPEE CUSHION IN MY DIAPER?

GIGGLE SNORT GIGGLE

HERE'S A GOOD ONE, BUNNY...WHAT'S ANOTHER NAME FOR "DIAPERS"?

"POTTY HOLDERS"

HAHAHAHA

STUFFED BUNNIES CAN BE A TOUGH AUDIENCE

IF YOU ASK ME, I THINK ALL THIS EMPHASIS ON PHYSICAL FITNESS IN TODAY'S FASHIONS IS GETTING OUT OF HAND

IT'S EVEN REACHED THE BABY LEVEL NOW...

"SWEAT DIAPERS"

JEFF MILLER! THAT'S YOUR THIRD PIECE OF CAKE TONIGHT

I CAN'T HELP IT. I'VE GOT A BIG SWEET TOOTH

RIGHT NOW I'D SETTLE FOR A LITTLE SOUR ONE

TOM ARMSTRONG

I'M REALLY STARTING TO GET A MID-YEARS' PAUNCH

I KNOW WHAT DAD MEANS...

I'M HAVING THE SAME PROBLEM WITH A MID-YEAR PUDGE

TOM ARMSTRONG

HMMM...MARVIN'S SPOTS SHOW ALL THE CLASSIC SIGNS OF BEING A RARE SKIN DISORDER KNOWN AS "DALMATION-ITIS"

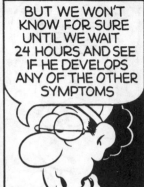

BUT WE WON'T KNOW FOR SURE UNTIL WE WAIT 24 HOURS AND SEE IF HE DEVELOPS ANY OF THE OTHER SYMPTOMS

TOM ARMSTRONG

SUCH AS...

WELL, FOR ONE THING, HE'LL GET AN OVER-WHELMING URGE TO RIDE ON THE BACK OF A FIRE TRUCK

I'VE ALREADY GOT AN URGE TO BITE HIM ON THE LEG

SOMETIMES A RASH LIKE MARVIN'S CAN BE CAUSED BY AN ALLERGY TO MILK PRODUCTS

PERHAPS IT WOULD BE A GOOD IDEA TO TAKE HIM OFF HIS FORMULA FOR A COUPLE OF WEEKS

CLUNK

DOCTOR! HE'S GOING INTO SHOCK!!

...AND WITHDRAWAL

TOM ARMSTRONG

I'M THE GOOD WITCH OF THE NORTH AND THIS IS "THE LAND OF BLAHS," MEAGAN

AND FOR GETTING RID OF THE WICKED WITCH OF THE EAST, THESE MAGICAL RED SHOES NOW BELONG TO YOU

WELL, HOW DO YOU LIKE THEM, MY DEAR?

I'M JUST NOT SURE...HAVE YOU GOT IT IN A NEON GREEN?

...AND I WAS WISHING SOMETHING EXCITING WOULD HAPPEN, WHEN SUDDENLY **ZAP!**— WE ENDED UP HERE

IT SOUNDS LIKE YOU NEED TO VISIT THE "WIZARD OF BLAHS." PERHAPS HE CAN HELP YOU WITH YOUR BOREDOM **Z**

JUST FOLLOW THAT YELLOW BRICK ROAD UNTIL YOU GET TO THE EMERALD CITY

"EMERALD CITY"? IT SOUNDS LIKE A DISCOUNT JEWELRY STORE

BOY, AM I GLAD YOU CAME ALONG, LITTLE GIRL

I WAS GROWING OLD WAITING FOR SOMEONE TO RESCUE ME FROM THIS CORNFIELD

WHY, JUST LOOK AT ALL MY CROW'S FEET

MY NAME IS MEAGAN, AND THIS IS MY DOG DODO

"DODO"?

WE'RE ON OUR WAY TO SEE THE WIZARD OF BLAHS. DO YOU WANT TO COME WITH US?

SURE, WHY NOT? SINCE I DON'T HAVE A BRAIN...

I CAN'T THINK OF ANYTHING BETTER TO DO

DO YOU THINK THE WIZARD WILL HELP US IF WE GET RID OF THE WICKED WITCH OF THE WEST?

WELL, IF YOU ASK ME, I THINK IT WAS **CRAZY** TO GO TO HIM

YEAH, MAYBE WE WERE ALL A LITTLE "OFF" TO SEE THE WIZARD

HEY! THAT'D MAKE A GREAT TITLE FOR A SONG!!

BOY, THE WICKED WITCH OF THE WEST SURE LIVES IN AN OUT-OF-THE-WAY PLACE

YEAH, I WISH THERE WAS SOME OTHER WAY TO GET TO HER CASTLE

I HATE FLYING ON THESE SMALL COMMUTER AIRLINES

I HATE THESE OLD HORROR MOVIES MOM WATCHES DURING MY LATE NIGHT FEEDINGS

EEEEEEEK!

ESPECIALLY THE MILK-CURDLING SCREAMS

TONIGHT'S LATE NIGHT HORROR MOVIE IS "KING KONG"

ROWRRR!

...IN 3-D

TOM ARMSTRONG

Y-Y-YOU'RE COUNT DRACULA!!

THAT'S RIGHT, MY LOVELY, BUT ALL MY FRIENDS CALL ME "WHITE FANG"

BECAUSE I ALWAYS BRUSH BETWEEN MEALS WITH "SHINE-UP" TOOTH-PASTE

THESE PRODUCT PLUGS IN MOVIES ARE DEFINITELY GETTING OUT OF HAND

TOM ARMSTRONG

AND NOW...

OH, BOY! THE "TONIGHT SHOW" IS COMING ON

TOM ARMSTRONG

...HEEEERE WAS JOHNNY!

RATS. IT'S A REPEAT

MAYBE I'M JUST BEING OLD-FASHIONED...

BUT WHENEVER I'M WATCHING TELEVISION WITH OTHER PEOPLE...

I ALWAYS GET EMBARRASSED WHEN A COMMERCIAL FOR DIAPER RASH CREAM COMES ON

...AND IF YOU ORDER TODAY, NOT ONLY WILL WE SEND YOU THIS SPECIAL DOUBLE RECORD COLLECTION OF "SLIM WHITMAN AND JULIO IGLESIAS SING BEETHOVEN"...

BUT WE'LL ALSO SEND YOU THIS HANDSOME SIMULATED OAK GUITAR PICK AT NO EXTRA CHARGE!! HERE'S HOW TO ORDER

AND NOW WE'LL RETURN YOU FOR A FEW BRIEF SECONDS TO OUR LATE NIGHT MOVIE PRESENTATION

Z   Z

TOM ARMSTRONG

HOW SWEET...

IN KEEPING WITH THE TRUE SPIRIT OF THE HOLIDAY SEASON...

BITSY HAS TAKEN IN A FAMILY OF HOMELESS FLEAS

THUMP! THUMP! THUMP!

BITSY

WAH!

WHAT'S THE MATTER, HONEY?

I JUST HAD A HORRIBLE DREAM

IT WAS ALL ABOUT A BUNCH OF THESE GIANT DANCING SUGAR PLUMS

LIGHT...

CAMERA...

...ACTION!!

RIIIP!
SHRED!
RIIIP!

CLICK

...Merry Christmas

TOM ARMSTRONG

I DON'T KNOW WHOSE IDEA IT WAS...

BUT IF YOU ASK ME, IT WAS A STROKE OF GENIUS...

TO START PUTTING BABY FORMULA IN 2-LITER BOTTLES

ARMSTRONG

I MUST ADMIT, JEFF, THAT WHEN WE WERE EXPECTING...

I WASN'T SURE HOW YOU WOULD ADJUST TO FATHERHOOD

BUT I'M REALLY PLEASED TO SEE YOU ADAPTING SO WELL TO YOUR NEW ROLE

Armstrong

THIS BABY FOOD TASTES LIKE STRAINED BLAH!

THERE'S ONLY ONE THING TO DO...

ADD KETCHUP

SPLOOT! SPLOOT!

Armstrong

SEE THE DAIRY COWS GRAZING IN THE PASTURE, MARVIN?

CHOMP!

IS THAT HOW YOU GET PASTURIZED MILK?

ARMSTRONG

I'VE REALLY STARTED FEELING OLD LATELY

I JUST DON'T SEEM TO HAVE MY USUAL PEP ANYMORE

I'VE EVEN NOTICED THAT I'M NOT AS LIGHT ON MY KNEES AS I USED TO BE

ARMSTRONG

WAIT'LL JENNY SEES THAT I'VE STARTED TO GROW A BEARD

NOTICE ANYTHING DIFFERENT ABOUT ME TODAY, JENNY?

SOMETHING THAT MAKES ME LOOK MORE MANLY? LET'S SEE...

YOU'VE GROWN A SECOND HAIR ON YOUR CHEST!

POOR DAD...EVER SINCE HE DECIDED TO GROW A BEARD, HE KEEPS CHECKING ITS PROGRESS IN THE MIRROR

RATS! IT JUST GOES TO PROVE THE OLD ADAGE...

A WATCHED BEARD NEVER GROWS

MOM THINKS THAT GRANDMA'S PAMPERING IS GOING TO RUIN ME

SO TODAY I'M DETERMINED TO RESIST ANY ATTEMPT TO CODDLE ME

LOOK, MARVIN, I MADE YOUR FAVORITE TREAT, CHOCOLATE CHIP COOKIES!

CURSES! SPOILED AGAIN!

ARMSTRONG

HERE, LET ME TAKE YOUR SHOES AND SOCKS OFF, MARVIN

AHHHHH... I LOVE TO PIGGY OUT!

ARMSTRONG

YOU KNOW, FLOPPET, I USED TO THINK GROWNUPS WERE DISCRIMINATING AGAINST BABIES BY NOT ALLOWING US TO QUALIFY FOR CREDIT

BUT AS I'VE GOTTEN OLDER, I'VE COME TO SEE THEY MAY HAVE SOME LEGITIMATE REASONS

FOR INSTANCE, BABIES HAVE A LONG HISTORY OF BEING CHRONICALLY UNEMPLOYED

I'M AFRAID ALL OF YOUR BABY BOTTLES ARE IN THE DISH-WASHER, MARVIN

...SO I HAD TO PUT YOUR MILK IN THIS SAUCER

WHAT DO I LOOK LIKE... A CAT ?!!

WHEN YOU LOOK OUT THE WINDOW IN THE SUMMER, THE SKY IS A BRILLIANT BLUE, THE GRASS IS AN IRISH GREEN AND FLOWERS ARE EVERYWHERE IN AN ARRAY OF DAZZLING HUES

BUT IN THE WINTER ALL YOU CAN GET IS A BLACK-AND-WHITE PICTURE

SOMETIMES IT SEEMS LIKE THERE JUST AREN'T ENOUGH HOURS IN THE DAY

I KNOW WHAT SHE MEANS...

SOME DAYS IT SEEMS AS IF I BARELY GET DONE WITH MY NAP AND IT'S TIME FOR BED

THAT'S WHAT I WANT TO BE WHEN I GROW UP...

A PROFESSIONAL WRESTLER

"BULK" MARVIN

TO BE A PROFESSIONAL WRESTLER, YOU'VE GOT TO BE ABLE TO INTIMIDATE YOUR OPPONENT

GRRRRR!

AS YOU CAN SEE... "FEARSOME" FLOPPET HAS BEEN RENDERED TOTALLY SPEECHLESS

I LOVE THIS PART OF A WRESTLING MATCH...

WHEN I THROW MY OPPONENT OUT OF THE RING

FLING!

WE PROFESSIONAL WRESTLERS HAVE RECEIVED A LOT OF BAD PRESS LATELY...

BUT ANYBODY WHO THINKS OUR MATCHES ARE ALL A FAKE...

HAS NEVER SEEN SOME OF THE HOLDS MOM PUTS ON ME WHEN IT'S TIME TO TAKE MY VITAMINS

A FAVORITE TRICK WE PRO WRESTLERS LIKE TO USE BEFORE A BIG MATCH...

IS TO TRY AND PSYCH-OUT OUR OPPONENT BY MAKING FUN OF HIS ANCESTRY

HEY, "DOGBREATH," YOUR OLD MAN WAS A CHIHUAHUA!

GRRRR!

YOU MAY BE TOUGH, "JAWBREAKER" JEFF, BUT NOT TOUGH ENOUGH TO DEFEAT "BULK" MARVIN!

BABY POWD

NEED SOME HELP WITH MARVIN, JEFF?

THANKS. YOU HOLD HIM DOWN WHILE I FINISH THE JOB

OH, NO...

BAB OWD

IT'S A TAG-TEAM MATCH!

LAST CHRISTMAS WE GAVE MARVIN A GREAT BIG TOY BOX

SO WHERE DOES HE KEEP ALL OF HIS TOYS?

IN MY BATHTUB!!

ARMSTRONG

SLURP! SLURP!

ARMSTRONG

LOOKS LIKE BITSY FELL ASLEEP ON THE HEAT REGISTER AGAIN

IT MUST BE EXCITING BEING THE FIRST ROBIN OF SPRING...

TRAVELING ALL OVER THE COUNTRY LETTING PEOPLE KNOW THAT WARM WEATHER IS COMING

IT'S NOT AS GLAMOROUS AS IT SOUNDS

IT GETS OLD RUSHING AROUND, GRABBING QUICK BITES BETWEEN FLIGHTS AND STAYING IN CHEAP NESTS EVERY NIGHT

YUP!...WE ROBINS ARE USUALLY ONE OF THE FIRST BIRDS BACK IN THE SPRING

PECK! PECK!

BUT YOU HAVE TO BE CAREFUL NOT TO RETURN *TOO* EARLY

...UNLESS, OF COURSE, YOU LIKE FROZEN DINNERS

ARMSTRONG

MR. ROBIN...

CALL ME ROB, KID

OKAY, ROB...I COULDN'T HELP NOTICING THAT YOUR CHEST IS ALL RED

YEAH, IT HAPPENS TO ME EVERY YEAR...

I ALWAYS FORGET TO USE A SUN BLOCK WHEN I'M IN FLORIDA

YOUR DAD MUST BE CHECKING TO SEE HOW MUCH DAMAGE THE COLD WEATHER DID TO THE LAWN

ACTUALLY, HE'S ESTIMATING HOW MANY MORE SATURDAYS HE'S GOT OFF BEFORE HE HAS TO START MOWING THE LAWN AGAIN

ARMSTRONG

WHAT DO YOU CALL THE EASTER BUNNY WHEN HE COMES A MONTH EARLY?

"THE **MARCH** HARE" YUCK! YUCK! YUCK!

ARMSTRONG—

VIS WIT

EAST BUN

I JUST LOVE **CRACKING** EASTER **YOLKS!**

YOU'LL FORGIVE ME IF I DON'T CRACK A SMILE

EASTE BUNI

AND JUST WHERE DO YOU THINK YOU'RE GOING LIKE THAT, YOUNG MAN?

YOU'RE SUPPOSED TO BE WEARING YOUR NEW EASTER SUIT FOR CHURCH

I COULD HAVE SWORN SHE SAID MY "BIRTHDAY SUIT"

ARMSTRONG—

...AND THIS IS THE OFFICE WATER COOLER, MARVIN

WOW! JUST THINK IF THAT BOTTLE WAS FULL OF MILK

ARMSTRONG

WHILE DAD'S BUSY WORKING

ARMSTRONG

I'LL JUST PLAY WITH HIS OFFICE COMPUTER

BEEP! BANG! BASH! BEEP BONK!

I HOPE THIS IS ONE OF THOSE ABUSER-FRIENDLY COMPUTERS

PAPER CARRIER "DEAD-EYE" DORA DROPS BACK INTO THE POCKET...

AND FIRES A PERFECT BULLET STRAIGHT FOR THE INTENDED PICTURE WINDOW

WAIT A MINUTE...IT LOOKS LIKE THERE MIGHT BE AN INTERCEPTION...

ARMSTRONG

OUR NEW PAPER CARRIER, "DEAD-EYE" DORA, SHOWS A REAL APTITUDE FOR BUSINESS

SHE'S ALREADY MADE SOME CHANGES DESIGNED TO IMPROVE THE EFFICIENCY OF HER PAPER ROUTE

SUCH AS SMOOTHER PRODUCT DISTRIBUTION

ARMSTRONG

OUCH!

I THINK THAT'S ENOUGH COLORING FOR ONE DAY

I'M STARTING TO GET SCRIBBLER'S CRAMP

I'M SURE YOU FOLKS WOULD BE VERY HAPPY WITH THIS LITTLE BABY IN YOUR HOME

SALE

OH, NO....!

THEY'RE GOING TO REPLACE ME WITH A DROID!!

HERE IN YOUR NURSERY, MARVIN, EVERYTHING SEEMS SO SAFE AND WARM

BUT OUTSIDE IN THE REAL WORLD IT'S A JUNGLE

I'VE NOTICED. WHEN ARE YOU EVER GOING TO GET AROUND TO MOWING THE LAWN?

ARMSTRONG

UH...WHAT'S WITH THE GET-UP, JENNY?

IT'S FOR SELF-PRESERVATION

MARVIN LEARNED HOW TO THROW TODAY

BONK!

ARMSTRONG

CHAPTER II

AFTER THE TRAUMA OF BIRTH, I WAS KIND OF OUT OF IT THAT FIRST DAY.

SCRIBBLE SCRIBBLE

BUT ON THE FOLLOWING DAY I GOT MY FIRST GOOD LOOK AT MY NEW DAD!

...AND SUFFERED A SECOND TRAUMA.

CHAPTER III

IT DIDN'T TAKE ME LONG TO NOTICE THAT WE BABIES IN THE NURSERY WERE DIVIDED INTO TWO GROUPS...

SCRIBBLE SCRIBBLE

THOSE WITH BLUE BLANKETS AND THOSE WITH PINK BLANKETS.

BUT AS FAR AS I COULD DISCERN, THAT WAS THE ONLY DIFFERENCE BETWEEN US.

CHAPTER IV
I WAS HAVING SOME TROUBLE ADJUSTING TO LIFE ON THE OUT-SIDE WORLD...

SCRIBBLE SCRIBBLE SCRIBBLE

UNTIL ONE OF THE NURSES GAVE ME SOMETHING TO HELP ME MAKE IT THROUGH THE NIGHT.

-ONLY 2 DAYS OLD AND ALREADY I HAD BECOME DEPENDENT ON A MIND-ALTERING SUBSTANCE.

SLURP! SLURP!

CHAPTER V
BY THE THIRD DAY, I WAS TOTALLY FED UP WITH ALL THE CRYING BABIES AROUND ME!

SCRIBBLE SCRIBBLE SCRIBBLE

I WAS READY TO WALK OUT OF THAT HOSPITAL!!

LUCKILY, MY MOM INSISTED ON CARRYING ME.

214

THERE'S ONLY ONE PERSON WHO CAN STOP THE FLOW OF ILLEGAL PACIFIERS INTO THIS COUNTRY...

MARVIN VICE

ARMSTRONG

SINCE DAD'S FIXING DINNER TONIGHT...

IT'S A GOOD THING I'M OLD ENOUGH FOR SOLID FOODS

WE'RE HAVING SOUP

ARMSTRONG

JEFF! MARVIN'S PLAYING IN THE SURF WITHOUT HIS SWIMSUIT!

DON'T WORRY HON, THE WAY THAT KID EATS...

THERE'S NO DANGER OF HIS BEING ARRESTED FOR SKINNY-DIPPING

ARMSTRONG

HEY, KID, LET'S MAKE A NEW RULE...

THE WINNER OF THE VOLLEYBALL GAME...

BOP!

BOP!

IS THE FIRST ONE TO GET THE BALL OVER THE NET

ARMSTRONG

Cartoonist Tom Armstrong is by no means a newcomer to the art field. At the ripe old age of five he drew a comic strip about camels, and from those humble beginnings sprang the comic genius behind Tom's later—and more human—syndicated cartoon creations, MARVIN and JOHN DARLING.

"I started cartooning probably before I could talk," Tom says. "My dad was an aspiring cartoonist, and after watching him for a while, I started drawing, too."

After four years of high school art training, Tom entered the University of Evansville, serving as the staff cartoonist for the campus paper, The Crescent, with a weekly strip about campus life called "Two-S." He graduated with a bachelor's degree in fine arts and several art awards under his belt: the Helen Morris Outstanding Senior Award in oil painting, the University of Evansville alumni Certificate of Excellence, the Medal of Merit for "significant contributions to collegiate journalism," second place for Best Editorial Cartoons from the Pi Delta Epsilon national journalism fraternity and the Indiana Collegiate Press Association's Best Editorial Cartoon award.

From there, Tom got into free-lance illustrating: He's drawn for many well-known publications, including **The Saturday Evening Post** and **The National Review**.

Tom has also done a good deal of work with advertising agencies, developing animated cartoons, multi-media slide presentations, animated TV spots and print ads for national companies from RCA to Sears and many more. He is a three-time recipient of the Golden Circle Award for "achieving the highest standards of advertising and selling excellence in worldwide competition."

Tom's first venture into comic strip syndication came in 1979 with JOHN DARLING, done in tandem with FUNKY WINKERBEAN creator Tom Batiuk. DARLING stars a fictional TV talk show host, his co-workers and celebrity guests (real-life celebrities drawn in caricature by Armstrong).

MARVIN, featuring the precocious red-haired star of Marvin Steps Out, followed in August, 1982. The character's popularity on the comics pages soon led to equal success in licensing and merchandising.

A prime-time television special, produced by Southern Star Studios, is in production for CBS.

Tom, his wife, Glenda, and two children, Jonathan and Jennifer (who also serve as a gold mine of ideas for MARVIN's antics) make their home in southern Indiana.